Pet Poems

also edited by Robert Fisher

AMAZING MONSTERS
Verses to Thrill and Chill

GHOSTS GALORE
Haunting Verse

FUNNY FOLK
Poems about People

WITCH WORDS
Poems of Magic and Mystery

ff

PET
POEMS

Edited by
Robert Fisher

Illustrated by
Sally Kindberg

faber and faber
LONDON · BOSTON

First published in 1989
by Faber and Faber Limited
3 Queen Square London WC1N 3AU

Photoset by Wilmaset, Birkenhead, Wirral
Printed in Great Britain by
Richard Clay, Bungay, Suffolk

British Library Cataloguing in Publication Data is available

ISBN 0–571–15248–1

Contents

Who are my pets ?

who are my pets
where can they be
look in the book
and you will see
a four-legged yapper
a shape-shifter
a body-changer
a little quaker
one ear up and one ear down
nuzzling and shuffling with a soft sucking sound
whole body trembling
darting eating parting meeting
cackle whistle roar and bark
often I want a whole Noah's Ark
who are my pets

2]   where can they be
look in the book
and you will see
the beauty of them all
so tall so small
right size bright eyes
looking very wise
dark as a stormcloud light as the sun
be friends to him and you'll have some fun
he looks so weak and little and slim
I pray the world will be good to him
if only you knew
you'd love him too
who are my pets
where can they be
look in the book
and you will see

Robert Fisher

There was a young lady named Maggie,
Whose dog was enormous and shaggy;
The front end of him
Looked vicious and grim –
But the back end was friendly and waggy.

Anon

Thin Dog

I've got a dog as thin as a rail,
He's got fleas all over his tail;
Every time his tail goes flop,
The fleas on the bottom all hop to the top.

Anon

The Hairy Dog

My dog's so furry I've not seen
His face for years and years:
His eyes are buried out of sight,
I only guess his ears.

When people ask me for his breed,
I do not know or care:
He has the beauty of them all
Hidden beneath his hair.

Herbert Asquith

Asleep he wheezes at his ease.
He only wakes to scratch his fleas.

He hogs the fire, he bakes his head
As if it were a loaf of bread.

He's just a sack of snoring dog.
You can lug him like a log.

You can roll him with your foot,
He'll stay snoring where he's put.

I take him out for exercise,
He rolls in cowclap up to his eyes.

He will not race, he will not romp,
He saves his strength for gobble and chomp.

He'll work as hard as you could wish
Emptying his dinner dish,

Then flops flat, and digs down deep,
Like a miner, into sleep.

Ted Hughes

Bad Dog

All day long, Bones hasn't been seen
– But now he comes slinking home
Smelling of ditches and streams
And pastures and pinewoods and loam
And tries to crawl under my bed.
His coat is caked with mud,
And one of his ears drips blood.
Nobody knows where he's been.

'Who did it?' they ask him, 'who . . .?
He'll have to be bathed . . . the sinner . . .
Pack him off to his basket . . .
You *bad dog*, you'll get no dinner . . .'
And he cowers, and rolls an eye.
Tomorrow, I *won't* let him go –
But he licks my hand, and then – oh,
How I wish that I had been too.

Brian Lee

Best friend?
Maybe!
Wiry hair-dropper,
four-legged yapper.
Sleep-disturber,
paws on the shoulders
and lick on the chin.
Unruly friend, sometimes.
I remember
Great Dane,
lolloping up stairs,
five-at-a-time
then sitting,
patient King of the Castle,
waiting for his slow
two-legged servant,
panting below.
Best friend!

Judith Nicholls

Dear God, I have a little dog,
He isn't really there, but in the night
When I'm alone I sometimes stroke his hair.
Dear God, I love my little dog who isn't really there,
So help him come out from my dreams
And let me keep him in my care.

Sophie Way, aged eight

Eight months ago, on Christmas Day,
he was a present for the twins,
a toy to join in all their play.

They left by car, but how long since
he cannot tell, nor when they'll come
(if ever) back, to make amends.

The house is blind and deaf and dumb,
the curtains drawn, the windows shut,
the doors sealed tighter than a tomb.

Even the little garden hut
is padlocked. He barks feebly at
each slowing car or passing foot.

Stretched on the WELCOME on the
    mat
in the front porch, he feels the hunger
gnawing inside him like a rat.

Suffers, endures, but knows no anger.

Raymond Wilson

Scat cat!
don't come back for more
there's a poor dead sparrow
by the kitchen door

Drat cat!
with your long sharp claw
took blood from the bird
that's left on the floor

Brat cat!
I'm not at all sure
I want you back
your slaughter's a bore

Fat cat!
eating fish that's raw
from your dish each day
you live by your law
and know no other way

Fancy that cat!
I should not ignore
that you're not just a pet
you're a hunter and more
you're my one true friend

So welcome back cat!
come and lick your paw
there's a fish in a dish
and a place to snore
you're the purr-fect cat for me

Robert Fisher

Pussy

I like little pussy, her coat is so warm;
And if I don't hurt her, she'll do me no harm.
So I'll not pull her tail, nor drive her away,
But pussy and I very gently will play.
She shall sit by my side, and I'll give her some food;
And she'll love me because I am gentle and good.

I'll pat pretty pussy, and then she will purr;
And thus show her thanks for my kindness to her.
But I'll not pinch her ears, nor tread on her paw,
Lest I should provoke her to use her sharp claw.
I never will vex her, nor make her displeased –
For pussy don't like to be worried and teased.

Anon c. 1830

Our old cat has kittens three –
What do you think their names should be?

One is a tabby, with emerald eyes,
   And a tail that's long and slender,
And into a temper she quickly flies
   If you ever by chance offend her:
      I think we shall call her this –
      I think we shall call her that –
Now, don't you think that Pepperpot
   Is a nice name for a cat?

One is black, with a frill of white,
   And her feet are all white fur, too;
If you stroke her she carries her tail upright
   And quickly begins to purr, too!
      I think we shall call her this –
      I think we shall call her that –
Now don't you think that Sootikin
   Is a nice name for a cat?

One is a tortoise-shell, yellow and black,
   With plenty of white about him;
If you tease him, at once he sets up his back:
   He's a quarrelsome one, ne'er doubt him.
      I think we shall call him this –
      I think we shall call him that –
Now don't you think that Scratchaway
   Is a nice name for a cat?

Our old cat has kittens three
And I fancy these their names will be;
Pepperpot, Sootikin, Scratchaway – there!
Were ever kittens with these to compare?
And we call the old mother –
      Now, what do you think?
Tabitha Longclaws Tiddley Wink.

Thomas Hood

My cat's tail
can dance or beckon
whilst he sleeps,
can wave or threaten,
fall or rise.

Warily
it lies awake,
all on its own;
he wakes,
it lies forgotten.
It lives a life alone,
quite separate –
or so it seems.

Could it be the place
where, secretly,
his life goes on?
A space to hide for ever
a million catty dreams?

Judith Nicholls

For I will consider my cat Jeoffry.

For he is the servant of the Living God, duly and daily serving him . . .

For first he looks upon his fore-paws to see if they are clean.

For secondly he kicks up behind to clear away there.

For thirdly he works it upon stretch with the fore-paws extended.

For fourthly he sharpens his paws by wood.

For fifthly he washes himself.

For sixthly he rolls upon wash.

For seventhly he fleas himself, that he may not be interrupted upon the beat.

For eighthly he rubs himself against a post.

For ninthly he looks up for his instructions.

For tenthly he goes in quest of food.

For having considered God and himself he will consider his neighbour

For if he meets another cat he will kiss her in kindness.

For when he takes his prey he plays with it to give it chance.

For one mouse in seven escapes by his dallying.

For when his day's work is done his business more properly begins.

For he keeps the Lord's watch in the night against the adversary.

For he counteracts the powers of darkness by his electrical skin and glaring eyes.

For he counteracts the Devil, who is death, by brisking about the life.

For in his morning orisons he loves the sun and the sun loves him.

For he is of the tribe of Tiger.

For the Cherub Cat is a term of the Angel Tiger.

For he has the subtlety and hissing of a serpent, which in goodness
he suppresses.
For he will not do destruction if he is well-fed, neither will he spit
without provocation.
For he purrs in thankfulness, when God tells him he's a good Cat.

Christopher Smart

Cat

My cat has got no name,
We simply call him Cat;
He doesn't seem to blame
Anyone for that.

For he is not like us
Who often, I'm afraid,
Kick up quite a fuss
If *our* names are mislaid.

As if, without a name,
We'd be no longer there
But like a tiny flame
Vanish in bright air.

My pet, he doesn't care
About such things as that:
Black buzz and golden stare
Require no name but Cat.

Vernon Scannell

Those who love cats which do not even purr,
Or which are thin and tired and very old,
Bend down to them in the street and stroke their fur
And rub their ears and smooth their breast, and hold
Their paws, and gaze into their eyes of gold.

                                        Francis Scarfe

The Rum Tum Tugger is a Curious Cat.
If you offer him pheasant he would rather have grouse.
If you put him in a house he would much prefer a flat,
If you put him in a flat then he'd rather have a house.
If you set him on a mouse then he only wants a rat,
If you set him on a rat then he'd rather chase a mouse.
Yes the Rum Tum Tugger is a Curious Cat –
   And there isn't any call for me to shout it:
     For he will do
     As he do do
       And there's no doing anything about it!

The Rum Tum Tugger is a terrible bore:
When you let him in then he wants to be out;
He's always on the wrong side of every door,
And as soon as he's at home, then he'd like to get about.
He likes to lie in the bureau drawer,
But he makes such a fuss if he can't get out.
Yes the Rum Tum Tugger is a Curious Cat –
   And there isn't any use for you to doubt it:
     For he will do
     As he do do
       And there's no doing anything about it!

The Rum Tum Tugger is a curious beast:
His disobliging ways are a matter of habit.
If you offer him fish then he always wants a feast;
When there isn't any fish then he won't eat rabbit.

If you offer him cream then he sniffs and sneers,
For he only likes what he finds for himself;
So you'll catch him in it right up to the ears,
If you put it away on the larder shelf.
The Rum Tum Tugger is artful and knowing,
The Rum Tum Tugger doesn't care for a cuddle;
But he'll leap on your lap in the middle of your sewing,
For there's nothing he enjoys like a horrible muddle.
Yes the Rum Tum Tugger is a Curious Cat –
  And there isn't any need for me to spout it:
    For he will do
    As he do do
      And there's no doing anything about it!

                        T. S. Eliot

I think that the tortoise-shell cat
Who lives with my aunt
Is a bewitched thing:
By no means, wholly, only, cat.
She's a shape-shifter, a body-changer,
Who in turn has been
Phoenix, mermaid, hippogriff.
Through feather and skin and scale
Her slit green eyes have seen
Glass mountains, emerald caves,
And the outer rims of space.
For this stately, crazy puss
Now roams for hours
On the soft South Downs,
In sheep's form, owl's plumes,
Under snail's shell, moth's wings.
My aunt calls her back
With a clack of her scissors.
Then quickly in cat's skin,
Amber runs home
To play with string, purr with fire,
If they're alone.
Crouched in anger and fear,
She hides when I'm there.
Aunt says she hates strangers.

Shirley Toulson

Old Hogan's goat was feeling fine,
Ate six red shirts from off the line.
Old Hogan grabbed him by the back
And tied him to the railroad track.

Now as the train came into sight,
The goat grew pale and green with fright.
He heaved a sigh as if in pain,
Coughed up those shirts and flagged the train.

Anon

Saint Jerome and his Lion

St Jerome in his study kept a great big cat,
It's always in the pictures, with its feet upon the mat.
Did he give it milk to drink in a little dish?
When it came to Fridays, did he give it fish?
If I lost my little cat I'd be sad without it,
I should ask St Jeremy what to do about it,
I should ask St Jeremy, just because of that,
For he's the only saint I know who kept a pussy cat.

Anon

I had a hippopotamus; I kept him in a shed
And fed him upon vitamins and vegetable bread;
I made him my companion on many cheery walks,
And had his portrait done by a celebrity in chalks.

His charming eccentricities were known on every side,
The creature's popularity was wonderfully wide;
He frolicked with the Rector in a dozen friendly tussles,
Who could not but remark upon his hippopotamuscles.

If he should be afflicted by depression or the dumps,
By hippopotameasles or the hippopotamumps,
I never knew a particle of peace till it was plain
He was hippopotamasticating properly again.

I had a hippopotamus; I loved him as a friend;
But beautiful relationships are bound to have an end.
Time takes, alas! our joys from us and robs us of our blisses;
My hippopotamus turned out a hippopotamissis.

My housekeeper regarded him with jaundice in her eye;
She did not want a colony of hippopotami;
She borrowed a machine-gun from her soldier-nephew, Percy
And showed my hippopotamus no hippopotamercy.

My house now lacks the glamour that the charming creature gave;
The garage where I kept him is as silent as the grave;
No longer he displays among the motor-tyres and spanners
His hippopotamastery of hippopotamanners.

No longer now he gambols in the orchards in the Spring;
No longer do I lead him through the village on a string;
No longer in the mornings does the neighbourhood rejoice
To his hippopotamusically-modulated voice.

I had a hippopotamus; but nothing upon earth
Is constant in its happiness or lasting in its mirth.
No joy that life can give me can be strong enough to smother
My sorrow for that might-have-been-a-hippopota-mother.

Patrick Barrington

As a friend to the children commend me the Yak.
    You will find it exactly the thing:
It will carry and fetch, you can ride on its back,
    Or lead it about with a string.

The Tartar who dwells on the plains of Thibet
    (A desolate region of snow)
Has for centuries made it a nursery pet,
    And surely the Tartar should know!

Then tell your papa where the Yak can be got,
    And if he is awfully rich
He will buy you the creature – or else he will not.
    (I cannot be positive which.)

Hilaire Belloc

I saw a donkey
One day old,
His head was too big
For his neck to hold;
His legs were shaky
And long and loose,
They rocked and staggered
And weren't much use.

He tried to gambol
And frisk a bit,
But he wasn't quite sure
Of the trick of it.
His queer little coat
Was soft and grey,
And curled at his neck
In a lovely way.

His face was wistful
And left no doubt
That he felt life needed
Some thinking about.
So he blundered round
In venturesome quest,
And then lay flat
On the ground to rest.

He looked so little
And weak and slim,
I prayed the world
Might be good to him.

Anon

My bull is white like the silver fish in the river,
White like the shimmering crane bird on the river bank,
White like fresh milk!
His roar is like thunder to the Turkish cannon on the steep shore.
My bull is dark like the rain cloud in the storm.
He is like summer and winter.
Half of him is dark like the storm cloud
Half of him is light like sunshine.
His back shines like the morning star.
His brow is red like the back of the hornbill.
His forehead is like a flag, calling the people from a distance.
He resembles the rainbow.
I will water him at the river,
With my spear I shall drive my enemies.
Let them water their herds at the well;
The river belongs to me and my bull.
Drink, my bull, from the river; I am here to guard you with my
   spear.

from *the Dinka*
Africa

They strolled down the lane together,
The sky was studded with stars –
They reached the gate in silence
And he lifted down the bars –
She neither smiled nor thanked him
Because she knew not how;
For he was just a farmer's boy
And she was a Jersey Cow.

Anon

Mary had a little lamb,
　　Its fleece was white as snow,
And everywhere that Mary went
　　The lamb was sure to go;
He followed her to school one day –
　　That was against the rule,
It made the children laugh and play
　　To see a lamb at school.

And so the teacher turned him out,
　　But still he lingered near,
And waited patiently about,
　　Till Mary did appear.
And then he ran to her and laid
　　His head upon her arm,
As if he said, 'I'm not afraid –
　　You'll shield me from all harm.'

'What makes the lamb love Mary so?'
　　The little children cry;
'Oh, Mary loves the lamb, you know,'
　　The teacher did reply,
'And you each gentle animal
　　In confidence may bind,
And make it follow at your call,
　　If you are always kind.'

Sarah Josepha Hale　　1788–1879

Mary had a little lamb,
'Twas awful dumb, it's true.
It followed her in a traffic jam,
And now it's mutton stew.

Anon

One white ear up,
One white ear down,
She nuzzles the wire
To be fed;
Sorrel she'll eat,
And burdock-leaves,
And cauliflower-stumps,
And bread;
But when all the nibbling
And twitching is done,
She settles back
On her straw;
For a rabbit likes
To squat in a hutch,
Not thinking much,
If at all.

That's how she behaves in company;
But what does she do when alone?
Has she sprightlier habits? Have tame white rabbits
A friskiness all their own?

Danny crept out
In dark of night,
When the grass was thick
With dew:
He scrabbled the wire

With his finger-nail,
And pushed a green
Leaf through;
But she would not stir
From her sleeping-end,
Nor rouse to his
Whispered call;

For a rabbit's life
Is to squat in a hutch,
Not thinking much,
If at all.

John Walsh

Mum won't let me keep a rabbit,
She won't let me keep a bat,
She won't let me keep a porcupine
Or a water-rat.

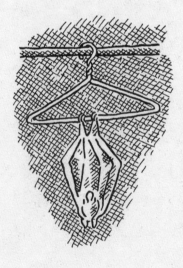

I can't keep pigeons
And I can't keep snails,
I can't keep kangaroos
Or wallabies with nails.

She won't let me keep a rattle-snake
Or viper in the house,
She won't let me keep a mamba
Or its meal, a mouse.

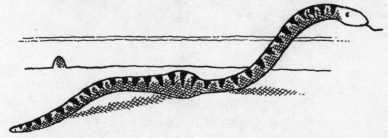

She won't let me keep a wombat
And it isn't very clear
Why I can't keep iguanas,
Jelly-fish or deer.

I can't keep a cockroach
Or a bumble-bee,
I can't keep an earwig,
A maggot or a flea.

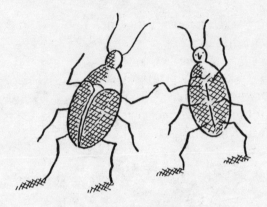

I can't keep a wildebeest
And it's just my luck
I can't keep a mallard,
A dabchick or a duck.

She won't let me keep piranhas,
Toads or even frogs,
She won't let me keep an octopus
Or muddy water-hogs.

So out in the garden I keep a pet ant
And up in the attic !TИAH933J3 T3ЯƆ3S A

Brian Patten

Here lies, whom hound did ne'er pursue,
   Nor swifter greyhound follow,
Whose foot ne'er tainted morning dew,
   Nor ear heard huntsman's hallo',

Old Tiney, surliest of his kind,
   Who, nurs'd with tender care,
And to domestic bounds confin'd,
   Was still a wild Jack-hare.

Though duly from my hand he took
   His pittance ev'ry night,
He did it with a jealous look,
   And, when he could, would bite.

His diet was of wheaten bread,
   And milk, and oats, and straw,
Thistles, or lettuces instead,
   With sand to scour his maw.

On twigs of hawthorn he regal'd,
   On pippins' russet peel;
And, when his juicy salads fail'd,
   Slic'd carrot pleas'd him well.

A Turkey carpet was his lawn,
   Whereon he lov'd to bound,
To skip and gambol like a fawn,
   And swing his rump around.

His frisking was at evening hours,
    For then he lost his fear;
But most before approaching show'rs,
    Or when a storm drew near.

Eight years and five round-rolling moons
    He thus saw steal away,
Dozing out all his idle noons,
    And ev'ry night at play.

I kept him for his humour' sake,
    For he would oft beguile
My heart of thoughts that made it ache,
    And force me to a smile.

But now, beneath this walnut-shade
    He finds his long, last home,
And waits in snug concealment laid,
    'Till gentler Puss shall come.

He, still more aged, feels the shocks
    From which no care can save,
And, partner once of Tiney's box,
    Must soon partake his grave.

William Cowper

Gentle rodent in its cage
Under the apple tree
It was a pet given to me
Named Poochie
Every day it squeaked
Ate anything it could get
Paper, grapes, grass and hay
It died early one morning
Garden its grave

Jake, aged eight

There was a little guinea-pig,
Who, being little, was not big;
He always walked upon his feet,
And never fasted when he eat.

When from a place he run away,
He never at the place did stay;
And while he run, as I am told,
He ne'er stood still for young or old.

He often squeaked, and sometimes violent,
And when he squeaked he ne'er was silent.
Though ne'er instructed by a cat,
He knew a mouse was not a rat.

One day, as I am certified,
He took a whim and fairly died;
And as I am told by men of sense,
He never has been living since.

Anon 1773

'A hedgehog is a creature with four legs, and thorns.'
That's what the roadman said,
So when I found one ambling uncertainly
On ridiculous, small feet, along the way
That's lined with dandelions and deadnettles
I thought: 'There's a hedgehog!
I wonder if he'll stay?'

We put out milk in a saucer.
Night by night
It disappeared. But we never saw him take it
Until once I came down swiftly
In pyjamas
Treading on each stair carefully –
Not to creak it –

And there he was, not alone, but with a trickle
Of wife and children wobbling after him
Scuffling their feet in the dark, wet grass.
I watched them
Nuzzling and snuffling at the saucer's brim
With a soft, sweet, sucking sound . . .

Next time I pass
Near the cinderpath with the dandelions
I shall look
For a creature with four legs, and thorns growing on it,
Wambling along like a hedge with no rose in it.
I might even write about him
In a book.

Jean Kenward

Once I had a gerbil –
Bought me by my Dad.
I used to watch it in its cage,
Running round like mad
Or sleeping in a corner
Nesting in a hole
Made of shavings, bits of wool
And chewed-up toilet roll.

I kept it in the kitchen
In the cage my cousin made.
It flicked all bits out on the floor
Mum grumbled – but it stayed.
I fed it; gave it water;
Was going to buy a wheel.
I used to take it out sometimes –
To stroke. I liked the feel –
All soft, with needle eyes,
A little throbbing chest.
I'd had a bird, a hamster too:
The gerbil I liked best.

I came downstairs one morning.
I always came down first.
In the cage there was no movement.

At once I knew the worst.
He lay there in the corner.
He'd never once been ill –

But now, fur frozen, spiky,
No throbbing, eye quite still.

I tell you – I just stood there
And quietly cried and cried,
And, when my Mum and Dad came down,
I said, 'My gerbil's died'.

And still I kept on crying,
Cried all the way to school,
But soon stopped when I got there
They'd all call me a fool.

I dawdled home that evening.
There, waiting, was my mother.
Said: 'Would you like another one?'
But I'll never want another.

John Kitching

Our hamster's life:
there's not much
to it,
not much
to it.

He presses his pink nose
to the door of his cage
and decides for the fifty-six
millionth time
that he can't get
through it.

Our hamster's life:
there's not much
to it,
not much
to it.

It's about the most boring
life in the world
if he only
knew it.
He sleeps and he drinks and he eats.
He eats and he drinks and he sleeps.

He slinks and he dreeps.
He eats.

This process
he repeats.

Our hamster's life:
there's not much
to it,
not much
to it.

You'd think it would drive him bonkers,
going round and round on his wheel.
It's certainly driving me bonkers,

watching him
do it.

But he may be thinking:
'That boy's life,
there's not much
to it,
not much
to it:

watching a hamster go round on a wheel,
It's driving me bonkers if he only knew it,

watching him
watching me
do it.'

Kit Wright

See him go
little scrabble rat
all of a fluster
sniffle-snitch
pink sweptback
ears a silk pucker

Gets into scuffles
gets no purchase
beats a blur on the walls
of his see-through cell
twitchy for a quick sip
suckles at his waterdrip

Snatches naps
in a newspaper heap
deconstructs
The Times to one-word scraps
shifting dune landscapes
of *and*s, *if*s and *but*s.

Set free
where would he go?
Ask the ink-black
hush-puss with her slow
slit-blink.
She knows.

Philip Gross

In a shoebox stuffed in an old nylon stocking
Sleeps the baby mouse I found in the meadow,
Where he trembled and shook beneath a stick
Till I caught him up by the tail and brought him in,
Cradled in my hand,

A little quaker, the whole body of him trembling,
His absurd whiskers sticking out like a cartoon mouse,
His feet like small leaves,
Little lizard-feet,
Whitish and spread wide when he tried to struggle away,
Wriggling like a minuscule puppy.

Now he's eaten his three kinds of cheese and drunk
    from his bottle-cap watering trough –

So much he just lies in one corner,
His tail curled under him, his belly big
As his head; his bat-like ears
Twitching, tilting towards the least sound.

Do I imagine he no longer trembles
When I come close to him?
He seems no longer to tremble.

                                        Theodore Roethke

He is not John the gardener,
   And yet the whole day long
Employs himself most usefully,
   The flower beds among.

He is not Tom the pussy cat,
   And yet the other day,
With stealthy stride and glistening eye,
   He crept upon his prey.

He is not Dash the dear old dog,
   And yet, perhaps, if you
Took pains with him and petted him,
   You'd come to love him too.

He's not a blackbird, though he chirps,
   And though he once was black;
And now he wears a loose grey coat,
   All wrinkled on the back.

He's got a very dirty face,
   And very shining eyes;
He sometimes comes and sits indoors;
   He looks – and p'r'aps is – wise.

But in a sunny flower bed
   He has a fixed abode:
He eats the things that eat my plants –
   He is a friendly TOAD.

Juliana Horatia Ewing

O
Wet
Pet!

Gyles Brandreth

O Goldfish!

I had a little goldfish that never seemed to end it swam all day in circles that drove me round and round and round and the round and round the round and round around and end round

Robert Fisher

I have a small aquarium
Where goldfish swim around –
Two little orange cheeky ones
They cost me just a pound
　　　(two weeks' pocket money).

I feed them each a ton of food.
They're sixteen metres long.
My Gran says they're an inch or two.
She's very, very wrong
　　　(as usual).

We have a lot of problems,
Including their fine size.
We took them down to London
For the Goldfish Enterprise
　　　(the Royal Goldfish Show).

The first judge said it was a shark.
The second judge agreed.
All the judges fled with fright.
My fish are a fine breed
　　　(as you know).

My goldfish were quite naughty.
They ate the smaller breed.
Luckily for me that day
I did not have to feed
　　　(the fish – of course).

My goldfish were on telly –
My fish were on the News.
No other goldfish in the world
Compared with them I'd choose
    (not one).

My goldfish are still growing –
Now eighteen metres long –
On telly in America,
On telly in Hong Kong
    (and other places too).

I have a large aquarium
Where goldfish swim around –
Two large and orange cheeky ones
They cost me just a pound
    (two weeks' pocket money).

Edward Williams, aged nine

Curving
 Curling
  Starting
   Stopping
    Swerving
     Upward
      Downward
       Dropping
       Squirming
      Gliding
     Darting
    Eating
   Worming
  Sliding
 Parting
Meeting!
Yet you say to me, a busy man,
'Do come and see my aquarium.'
I can't. It's too exhausting.

Spinning
  Pouting
   Inning
    Outing
     Squiggling
      Wriggling
      Nidding
       Nodding
       Looping
      Lurching
     Swooping
    Searching
   Gyring
  Never
  Never
 Tiring!
And still you say to me, a harassed man,
'Do come and see my aquarium.'
I can't. It's too exhausting.

Christopher Hassall

One night in thunder,
Two newts came to our back door to shelter
From the torrential rain and gusty wind;
I found them there when the rain had passed.
I caught them and kept them.
They are small and squirm when they are picked up.
Their stomachs and breasts are orange and black,
Pulsing with life.
They have four webbed feet and long shiny tails;
They are elegantly exact when they swim.

Out of the thunder night,
Came my black and orange dragons.

Clarissa Hinsley, aged twelve

I had a pet lizard called Albert,
Now one night he was very naughty
He got loose and we couldn't find him
Until mummy got into bed,
And then you can guess what happened.
She jumped out of bed with a scream.
That was the end of poor Albert.
Nothing could make mummy change her mind.

Jasmine Pinto, aged twelve

The Python

A Python I should not advise, –
It needs a doctor for its eyes,
And has the measles yearly.

However, if you feel inclined
To get one (to improve your mind,
And not from fashion merely),

Allow no music near its cage;
And when it flies into a rage
Chastise it, most severely.

I had an aunt in Yucatan
Who bought a Python from a man
And kept it for a pet.

She died, because she never knew
These simple little rules and few; –
The Snake is living yet.

Hilaire Belloc

I love my little gecko
And wonder whether he
My sentiments would echo
If he could talk to me

Colin West

I had a sweet tortoise called Pye
Wabbit.
He ate dandelions, it was
His habit.
Pye Wabbit, Pye Wy-et,
It was more than a habit, it was
His diet.
All the hot summer days, Pye
Wy-et, Pye Wiked-it,
Ate dandelions. I lay on the grass flat to see
How much he liked it.
In the autumn when it got cold, Pye Wiked-it, Pye
Wy-bernator,
Went to sleep till next spring. He was
a hibernator.
First he made a secret bed for the winter,
To lie there.
We loved him far too much ever
To spy where.
Why does his second name change every time?
Why, to make the rhyme.
Pye our dear tortoise
Is dead and gone.
He lies in the tomb we built for him, called
'Pye's Home'.
Pye, our dear tortoise,
We loved him so much.
Is he as dear to you now
As he was to us?

Stevie Smith

You know what it is to be born alone
Baby tortoise!

The first day to heave your feet little by little from the shell,
Not yet awake,
And remain lapsed on earth,
Not quite alive.

A tiny, fragile, half-animate bean.

To open your tiny beak-mouth, that looks as if it would never
    open,
Like some iron door;
To lift the upper hawk-beak from the lower base
And reach your skinny little neck
And take your first bite at some dim bit of herbage,
Alone, small insect,
Tiny bright-eye,
Slow one.

                                        D. H. Lawrence

Why, O why,
did you make me cry?
The angry words you said
keep echoing in my head,
and all because I did not feed
my budgie with his breakfast seed.

For all your alarm,
he has come to no harm,
has been happy all day
singing my tears away;
does not look sad or thin
though I put no water in his tin,
or gave him fresh sand,
so, why can't you understand
we all make mistakes?
And, O, how my heart aches
that I neglected my bird;
but don't say another word,
just go through the door,
leave me alone,
to grieve on my own;
I don't want you to see
my misery.

He's there in the kitchen now
like any bird on bough,
the whole house he fills
with his wonderful trills;
glad to be home with us,
he does not grumble or fuss.

Leonard Clark

The Emu makes, though prone to fret,
A quite accommodating pet.
By dint of arduous explaining –
And tactful and intensive training
It may be taught a mild routine
To lighten the domestic scene –
To peg the clothes – to draw a phaeton –
To greet such guests it has to wait on –
To tile the roof – to polish floors
And other preferential chores.
In doing jobs like these, the Emu
Will grow to cherish and esteem you.

Leon Gellert

No mother! No father!
Come little sparrow
Play with me

Issa

The bird in the cage
How sadly he watches
The butterflies

Issa

I had a dove and the sweet dove died;
   And I have thought it died of grieving.
O, what could it grieve for? Its feet were tied,
   With a silken thread of my own hand's weaving.
Sweet little red feet! why did you die –
Why would you leave me, sweet bird! why?
     You lived alone on the forest tree,
Why, pretty thing, could you not live with me?
I kiss'd you oft and gave you white peas;
Why not live sweetly, as in the green trees?

John Keats

What can it be
This curious anxiety?
It is as if I wanted
To fly away from here.

But how absurd!
I have never flown in my life,
And I do not know
What flying means, though I have heard,
Of course, something about it.

Why do I peck the wires of this little cage?
It is the only nest I have ever known.
But I want to build my own,
High in the secret branches of the air.

I cannot quite remember how
It is done, but I know
That what I want to do
Cannot be done here.

I have all I need –
Seed and water, air and light.
Why, then, do I weep with anguish,
And beat my head and my wings
Against these sharp wires, while the children
Smile at each other, saying: 'Hark how he sings'?

James Kirkup

Then the little Hiawatha
Learned of every bird its language,
Learned their names and all their secrets;
How they built their nests in Summer,
Where they hid themselves in Winter,
Talked with them whene'er he met them,
Called them 'Hiawatha's Chickens'.

Of all beasts he learned the language,
Learned their names and all their secrets,
How the beavers built their lodges,
How the squirrels hid their acorns,
How the reindeer ran so swiftly,
Why the rabbit was so timid;
Talked with them whene'er he met them,
Called them 'Hiawatha's Brothers'.

Henry Wadsworth Longfellow
from *The Song of Hiawatha*

It was high summer.
Age nine I travelled alone
to stay at Gran's.
'ello 'ello 'ello 'ello
screeched her green parrot
when I entered the front room
and gazed up at the huge cage
perched high on a wooden pedestal.

That amazing parrot!
Its shrill whistle
could pierce your eardrum.
It scattered sunflower seeds
halfway across the carpet
and then climbed around
and around its cage
cackling like a crackpot!

'oo's that? 'oo's that?
it squealed when my father
arrived to take me home.
Just watch this, said Dad,
and poked his finger at the cage.
The parrot raced along its perch
and flew at him in a rage.
Dad's finger jabbed closer, closer.

Furious, Gran's green parrot shrieked
at that teasing finger
until, like lightning,
it struck at Dad's flesh.
That black beak . . . wearing blood-red lipstick!
Dad tore around and around
Gran's front room
hollering like a hooligan!

Wes Magee

One day at a Perranporth pet-shop
   On a rather wild morning in June,
A lady from Par bought a budgerigar
   And she sang to a curious tune:
'Say that you love me, my sweetheart,
   My darling, my dovey, my pride,
My very own jewel, my dear one!'
   'Oh lumme,' the budgie replied.

'I'll feed you entirely on cream-cakes
   And doughnuts all smothered in jam,
And puddings and pies of incredible size,
   And peaches and melons and ham.
And you shall drink whiskies and sodas,
   For comfort your cage shall be famed.
You shall sleep in a bed lined with satin.'
   'Oh crikey!' the budgie exclaimed.

But the lady appeared not to hear him
   For she showed neither sorrow nor rage,
As with common-sense tardy and action foolhardy
   She opened the door of his cage.
'Come perch on my finger, my honey,
   To show you are mine, O my sweet!' –
Whereupon the poor fowl with a shriek and a howl
   Took off like a jet down the street.

And high he flew up above Cornwall
  To ensure his escape was no failure,
Then his speed he increased and he flew south and east
  To his ancestral home in Australia.
For although to the Australian abo
  The word 'budgerigar' means 'good food',
He said, 'I declare I'll feel much safer there
  Than in Bodmin or Bugle or Bude.'

ENVOI
And I'm sure with the budgie's conclusion
  You all will agree without fail:
Best eat frugal and free in a far-distant tree
  Than down all the wrong diet in jail.

Charles Causley

The Canary

Mary had a little bird,
  With feathers bright and yellow,
Slender legs – upon my word,
  He was a pretty fellow!

Sweetest notes he always sung,
  Which much delighted Mary;
Often where his cage was hung,
  She sat to hear Canary.

Crumbs of bread and dainty seeds
  She carried to him daily,
Seeking for the early weeds,
  She decked his palace gaily.

This, my little readers, learn,
  And ever practice duly;
Songs and smiles of love return
  To friends who love you truly.

Elizabeth Turner   1775–1846

When I have a beard that's curly and weird,
I'll buy myself a peacock bird.
He'll shout, 'Hello, hello, hello,'
As on my lawns he'll to and fro.
Other birds will hop and glare
As he sheds feathers here and there.

I'll ask my Aunty Maud to tea
(For she has swans and a maple tree)
To view my peacock on my lawn
Who shouts 'Hello' from break of dawn,
And spy his mantle spreading wide
All shimmering blue and golden-eyed.

Modwena Sedgwick

There was never a Queen like Balkis,
From here to the wide world's end;
But Balkis talked to a butterfly
As you would talk to a friend.

There was never a King like Solomon,
Not since the world began;
But Solomon talked to a butterfly
As a man would talk to a man.

She was the Queen of Sabaea,
And *he* was Asia's Lord –
But they both of 'em talked to butterflies
When they took their walks abroad!

                                    Rudyard Kipling

If you ever come to our house,
Keep your parents out of sight,
Or my sister's little monster,
Will devour them in one bite!

My sister's little monster,
Ate my aunty for its tea,
And my uncle for its dinner,
But it couldn't catch me!

My sister's little monster,
Lives among the raspberry canes,
I don't know what it is,
But I avoid it just the same!

Carolyn Gardner, aged thirteen

My Obnoxious Brother Bobby

My obnoxious brother Bobby
Has a most revolting hobby;
There behind the garden wall is
Where he captures creepy-crawlies.

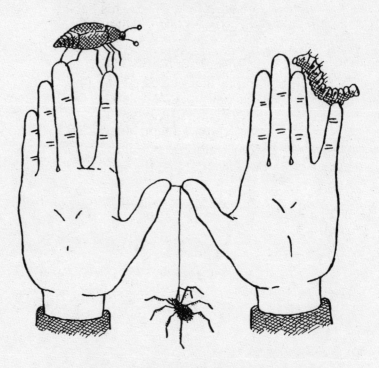

Grannies, aunts and baby cousins
Come to our house in their dozens,
But they disappear discreetly
When they see him smiling sweetly.

For they know, as he approaches,
In his pockets are cockroaches,
Spiders, centipedes and suchlike;
All of which they do not much like.

As they head towards the lobby,
Bidding fond farewells to Bobby,
How they wish he'd change his habits
And keep guinea pigs or rabbits.

But their wishes are quite futile,
For he thinks that bugs are cute. I'll
Finish now, but just remind you:
Bobby could be right behind you!

Colin West

My dragon's name is Jocelyn,
He's something of a joke.
For Jocelyn is very tame,
He doesn't like to maul or maim,
Or breathe a fearsome fiery flame;
He's much too smart to smoke.

And when I take him to the park
The children form a queue,
And say, 'What lovely eyes of red!'
As one by one they pat his head.
And Jocelyn is so well-bred,
He only eats a few!

Colin West

My animals are made of wool and glass,
Also of wood. Table and mantlepiece
Are thickly covered with them. It's because
You cannot keep real cats or dogs in these

High up new flats. I really want to have
A huge soft marmalade or, if not that,
Some animal that seems at least to love,
Hamsters? A dog? No, what I need's a cat.

I hate a word like 'pets'. It sounds so much
Like something with no living of its own.
And yet each time that I caress and touch
My wool or glass ones, I feel quite alone.

No kittens in our flat, no dog to bark
Each time the bell rings. Everything is still.
Often I want a zoo, a whole Noah's Ark.
Nothing is born here, nothing tries to kill.

Elizabeth Jennings

My Pet Koala

I have a pet koala
he is all fluffy and grey
and he is missing an eye
when Mummy put him
in the washing machine
he has one black eye
it is a pity
he's stuffed

Tom, aged five

Cold blood or warm, crawling or fluttering
Bric-à-brac, all are here to be bought,
Noisy or silent, python or myna,
Fish with long silk trains like dowagers,
Monkeys lost to thought.

In a small tank tiny enamelled
Green terrapin jostle, in a cage a crowd
Of small birds elbow each other and bicker
While beyond the ferrets, eardrum, eyeball
Find that macaw too loud.

Here behind glass lies a miniature desert,
The sand littered with rumpled gauze
Discarded by snakes like used bandages;
In the next door desert fossilized lizards
Stand in a pose, a pause.

But most of the customers want something comfy –
Rabbit, hamster, potto, puss –
Something to hold on the lap and cuddle
Making believe it will return affection
Like some neutered succubus.

Purr then or chirp, you are here for our pleasure,
Here at the mercy of our whim and purse;
Once there was the wild, now tanks and cages,
But we can offer you a home, a haven,
That might prove even worse.

Louis MacNeice

On shallow straw, in shadeless glass,
Huddled by empty bowls, they sleep:
No dark, no dam, no earth, no grass –
Mam, get us one of them to keep.

Living toys are something novel,
But it soon wears off somehow.
Fetch the shoebox, fetch the shovel –
Mam, we're playing funerals now.

Philip Larkin

A squirrel is digging up the bulbs
In half the time Dad took to bury them.

A small dog is playing football
With a mob of boys. He beats them all,
Scoring goals at both ends.
A kangaroo would kick the boys as well.

Birds are so smart they can drink milk
Without removing the bottle-top.

Cats stay clean, and never have to be
Carried screaming to the bathroom.
They don't get their heads stuck in railings,
They negotiate first with their whiskers.

The gecko walks on the ceiling, and
The cheetah can outrun the Royal Scot.
The lion cures his wounds by licking them,
And the guppy has fifty babies at a go.

The cicada plays the fiddle for hours on end,
And a man-size flea could jump over St Paul's.

If ever these beasts should get together
Then we are done for, children.
I don't much fancy myself as a python's pet,
But it might come to that.

D. J. Enright

Acknowledgements

The editor is grateful for permission to use the following copyright material:

'I Had a Hippopotamus' by Patrick Barrington, reproduced by permission of *Punch*.

'The Yak' and 'The Python' from *Cautionary Verses* by Hilaire Belloc, published by Gerald Duckworth & Co. Ltd.

'Ode to a Goldfish' by Gyles Brandreth, by permission of the author.

'Grumblers' by Leonard Clark, by permission of Robert A. Clark.

'One day at a Perranporth Pet-shop' from *Figgie Hobbin* by Charles Causley, published by Macmillan.

'The Rum Tum Tugger' from *Old Possum's Book of Practical Cats* by T. S. Eliot, published by Faber and Faber Ltd.

'Better Be Kind to Them Now' from *Collected Poems* by D. J. Enright, published by Oxford University Press, reproduced by permission of Watson Little Ltd.

'Verbal Gerbil' by Philip Gross, by permission of the author.

'Tropical Fish' from *Here be Lions* by Christopher Hassall, published by Cambridge University Press.

'My Newts' by Clarissa Hinsley, from *Children as Poets*, published by William Heinemann Ltd, by permission of Cambridgeshire Education Authority.

'Roger the Dog' from *What is the Truth?* by Ted Hughes, published by Faber and Faber Ltd.

'My Animals' from *My Secret Brother* by Elizabeth Jennings, published by Macmillan.

'The Composition' by Jean Kenward, by permission of the author.

'The Caged Bird in Springtime' from *A Spring Journey and Other Poems* by James Kirkup, published by Oxford University Press.

'My Gerbil' by John Kitching, by permission of the author.

'Take One Home for the Kiddies' from *The Whitsun Weddings* by Philip Larkin, published by Faber and Faber Ltd.

'Bad Dog' from *Late Home* by Brian Lee, published by Kestrel Books.

'Pet Shop' from *The Collected Poems of Louis MacNeice* by Louis MacNeice, published by Faber and Faber Ltd.

'Gran's Green Parrot' by Wes Magee, by permission of the author.

'Cat' and 'Dog' from *Midnight Forest* by Judith Nicholls, published by Faber and Faber Ltd.

'Mum Won't Let Me Keep a Rabbit' from *Gargling with Jelly* by Brian Patten, published by Kestrel Books.

'I had a pet lizard' by Jasmine Pinto from *Cats (and other crazy cuddlies)* edited by Richard and Helen Exley, © Exley Publications Ltd.

'The Meadow Mouse' from *The Collected Poems of Theodore Roethke* by Theodore Roethke, published by Faber and Faber Ltd.

'Cat' by Vernon Scannell, by permission of the author.

'Cats' from *Underworlds* by Francis Scarfe, published by William Heinemann Ltd.

'My Tortoise' from *The Collected Poems of Stevie Smith* by Stevie Smith, published by Penguin Books Ltd.

'Amber' from *Over the Bridge* by Shirley Toulson, published by Kestrel Books.

'Hoping for a Dog' by Sophie Way, from *Dogs (and other furry funnies)* edited by Richard and Helen Exley, © Exley Publications Ltd.

'The White Rabbit' by John Walsh, by permission of Mary Walsh.